When 10-year-old Ben Tennyson stumbles upon a mysterious alien device in the woods one summer, little does he realise that his life is set to change - forever.

As soon as the watch-like Omnitrix quite literally gets a grip on him, Ben discovers it gives him the ability to transform into 10 different alien super-beings, each one with awesome powers!

Using the Omnitrix to cause super-powered mischief turns out to be fun, but will Ben learn to use his might to fight for good?

READ ON AND FIND OUT . . .

EGMONT
We bring stories to life

Published in Great Britain 2009
by Egmont UK Limited
239 Kensington High Street, London W8 6SA

Ben 10 and all related characters and elements
are trademarks of and © Cartoon Network.
(s09)

Adapted from the animated series by
Barry Hutchison

1 3 5 7 9 10 8 6 4 2

A CIP catalogue record for this title is available from
the British Library

Printed and bound in Great Britain by the CPI Group

CHAPTER ONE

THE FURY OF FOUR ARMS!

On a busy street in downtown San Francisco, Gwen and Grandpa Max stood in a queue, fidgeting impatiently. In front of them, Ben waited quietly, his eyes fixed on the video-game store up ahead. Behind them, the queue seemed to stretch on forever.

'We've been in this line for *two hours*,' complained Gwen, 'and it hasn't budged an inch!'

Ben didn't take his eyes off the front door of the game shop. 'Small price to pay for *Sumo Slammers Two-point-one!*' he told her. 'I'd do anything to get this game – even be seen in public with you!'

'Don't you already have this stupid video game?'

'*Hello!*' Ben scoffed, turning to face her. 'This is *Sumo Slammers Two-point-one*. You can change your fighter's colour at any time during the match. *Duh!*'

'You know, there is a nice air-conditioned bookstore over there,' said Grandpa, diplomatically. 'Maybe we could wait inside until the line thins out a bit.'

'And lose my place?' gasped Ben. 'Not an option. You two go. I'll get my game and meet you guys back at the motorhome.'

They didn't need telling twice. Before Ben could change his mind, Grandpa and Gwen broke from the line and started towards the bookstore.

'Want us to pick anything up for you?' asked Grandpa.

Ben frowned. 'I'm on summer vacation. Why would I read anything?'

Hours later, having spent the afternoon browsing
the aisles of the bookshop, Gwen and Grandpa
stepped out into the San Francisco sunshine.

'So,' said Gwen with a grin, 'think Ben's
gone stir crazy in that line yet?'

KA-RAAASH!

Grandpa and Gwen shielded their eyes
as the front windows of the video-game shop
exploded outwards, showering the area with

deadly shards of glass. A second later, a large, familiar figure leaped out into the street. He clutched a bundle of *Sumo Slammers 2.1* video games in his arms. His *four* arms.

With sirens wailing, a police car skidded round the corner and sped towards the giant red brute. As it neared him, Four Arms reached down and scooped the vehicle up. He shook the car violently until the two policemen inside came tumbling out. They both ran away screaming. They weren't being paid enough to deal with aliens!

'Uh, why is Ben going berserk and tossing around police officers?' asked Gwen, barely able to believe her eyes.

Grandpa could only shake his head and shrug. 'Good question.'

A sound like the whirring of a giant fan split the air overhead. Grandpa and Gwen looked up to see a helicopter swooping down. A TV news cameraman leaned out through the side door, capturing all the action on film.

The helicopter banked sharply as a flying lamp post shot up towards it like a javelin. The metal pole narrowly missed, then curved back down towards the ground. Grandpa yanked his granddaughter out of the way, just as the lamp post clattered down where she had just stood.

Four Arms spun, fists raised, as a whole platoon of police cars screamed towards him. Snarling, he caught the front of a nearby parked car and threw it up into the air. It flipped end over end, before smashing into the approaching police vehicles.

'He must've snapped his gap,' Gwen gasped. 'All this for a video game!'

'I don't believe it,' muttered her grandfather. Ben would never behave like this. Would he?

A sleek, black armoured car pulled up beside the Tennysons, its powerful engine humming quietly. They watched, intrigued, as four mean-looking men stepped out. They brushed past Grandpa and Gwen, looking for the nearest police officer. They found him cowering behind a mail box.

'Lieutenant Steel, Special Alien Containment Team,' said the largest of the men, flashing the officer his ID badge. 'We'll take it from here.'

Not bothering to wait for a reply, Steel turned to his men and barked: 'Concussion Bazooka!'

The closest soldier leaned inside the armoured vehicle. When he emerged, an enormous cannon was mounted on his shoulder.

'This doesn't look good.' Grandpa gulped as he watched the man take aim. Before he could stop her, Gwen ducked past the containment team and sprinted across to Four Arms, who was still tearing the street to pieces.

'Ben, what are you doing?' she demanded.

A large shadow passed over Gwen as Four Arms threw back his powerful fists and brought them down towards her head. She opened her mouth to scream, but the sound was drowned out by the electronic whine of the Concussion Bazooka.

The blast slammed into Four Arms like an express train. It lifted him off his feet and sent him crashing through the front wall of a restaurant on the other side of the street.

'Ben!' Grandpa cried, running up and throwing a protective arm round Gwen.

Dust and smoke poured from inside the

ruined remains of the restaurant, but nothing else moved. Gwen and Grandpa watched, barely daring to breathe, both silently praying for some sign that Ben was alive.

Then, something shifted in the shadows of the shattered shop front. A shape – much larger than any human – stepped through the choking smoke. Everyone watching saw it twist at the waist. They heard it give a grunt of effort. They saw a pizza oven arc across the sky, flames flickering deep within it.

With a deafening **BOOM** the oven hit a parked van and exploded like a bomb. A wall of flame erupted from within it, setting light to everything close by.

As police and civilians alike ran for cover, Four Arms threw up his fists and roared with rage. Grandpa and Gwen could only stand by and watch as the mighty alien tensed his powerful leg muscles, then leaped off over the rooftops.

Grandpa Max glanced around at the utter destruction Four Arms had left in his wake. Ben couldn't have done this. There had to be another explanation for what had just happened.

There had to be!

�֍ ✖ ✖

Gwen yanked open the door of The Rust Bucket and flew up the steps in a single bound. Her face was red with rage.

'Are you demented?' she shrieked when she saw Ben sitting at the table. 'Going alien just to get a stupid video game!'

Ben glanced up briefly from his hand-held games console. 'What are you talking about?' he asked, frowning.

'You going four-arm-freaky in front of that store, that's what I'm talking about!'

'Now, I'm sure he has a good explanation,'

said Grandpa as he came up the stairs. He looked over at his grandson hopefully. 'Don't you, Ben?'

'Yeah.' Ben nodded, turning his attention back to *Sumo Slammers 2.1*. 'I don't know what you're talking about. I haven't done anything wrong.'

'Oh, yeah?' Gwen flicked on the motorhome's small TV screen. Ben looked up and found himself watching Four Arms smashing up police cars.

'That's not me!' Ben protested.

'Oh, no, I'm sure it's just some *other* four-armed alien going crazy in front of a video-game store!'

'It's possible,' said Ben. 'All the alien species in the watch live out in the universe somewhere.'

'That's true,' Grandpa agreed. 'Besides, Ben wouldn't be so irresponsible with his alien powers like that.'

'Grandpa, *please*,' scoffed Gwen.

The old man thought about his last comment for a moment. 'All right,' he told Gwen, 'maybe you have a point.'

Ben set his console down on the table and got to his feet. The game would have to wait. Some things were even more important than *Sumo Slammers*.

Squeezing past Grandpa, Ben threw open the door and stomped out of The Rust Bucket.

'No one ruins my alien's reputation,' he seethed. 'Except *me!*'

CHAPTER TWO

FAMILIAR FACES

Ben picked his way through the debris outside the video-game store. The street looked like World War III had hit it. Wrecked remains of cars lay burning on the road. Huge chunks of brickwork had crumbled from shop fronts, smashing holes in the pavement where

they'd landed. It was going to take a long time to clean this mess up.

'A criminal always returns to the scene of the crime,' said Gwen, walking behind her cousin.

'Will you give it a rest?' Ben replied. 'I'm trying to solve a mystery here.'

'What do you expect to find that everyone else couldn't?' asked Grandpa.

A movement in the shadows of an alleyway caught Ben's eye. There, lurking at the far end of the narrow passage, was a monstrous shape with four powerful arms.

'There he is!' The figure ducked round a corner and Ben set off after him. As he sprinted along the alley, Ben spun the dial on the Omnitrix, searching for the high-speed hero, XLR8. Running made it difficult to see which alien form he was selecting though, so rather than risk changing into Grey Matter, he decided just to stay himself.

An out-of-breath Ben staggered out of the other end of the alleyway, his chest aching from the effort of the chase. A big red shape paused on the roof of a nearby building before disappearing inside.

Ben's eyes narrowed as he read the sign above the door of the grand, imposing building.

'The Mint!' he gasped. The fake Four Arms had just broken into a building where huge amounts of money were printed. That could only be bad news!

As Ben charged off in the direction of the US Mint building, Grandpa and Gwen skidded out of the alley behind him. Grandpa stumbled along unsteadily, barely able to keep up with his speeding grandchildren.

He stopped for a moment to catch his breath and wipe the sweat from his brow. 'Who said,' he gasped, 'that retirement was relaxing?'

❈ ❈ ❈

A few moments later, Grandpa, now able to breathe, sneaked into the main printing room of the Mint with Gwen. Long sheets of paper whizzed through printers – going in blank and emerging as hundreds of millions of dollars. Coins slid from stamping machines into transport trolleys, their metal still hot to the touch. But Ben was nowhere to be seen.

'Are you *sure* he came in here?' asked Grandpa.

As if in answer to his question, a huge fireball lit up the room. Grandpa and Gwen darted round a corner to find Heatblast scaring off two security guards with a jet of flickering flame.

'OK, I was willing to give him one,' Gwen seethed, 'but two of Ben's aliens terrorising San Francisco? That can't be a coincidence, Grandpa. I'm stopping this right now!' Not waiting for a reply, she turned and stomped off towards the fiery alien.

'Yo, hothead,' she cried, 'back off the fireworks before someone gets hurt.' She glared up at Heatblast and folded her arms in front of her. 'Now, if you take responsibility for all the whacko stuff you've been doing lately, I'm sure we can help you.'

'Uh, Gwen,' came a voice from behind her.

'Not now, dweeb,' she sighed. 'Can't you see I've got a . . .' Her voice trailed off as she realised who the voice belonged to. 'Ben?' But, if her cousin was behind her, that meant . . .

'So, who are you?' she asked, taking a

step away from the fake Heatblast.

'Me?' growled the alien, his hands turning white with heat as he spoke. 'I'm a hottie, can't you tell?'

A plume of flame leaped from his fingertips. Gwen closed her eyes, unable to get out of the way in time. She heard something heavy hitting the ground in front of her. When she opened her eyes again, Diamondhead stood before her, shielding her from the fire.

'*Now* do you believe me?' Ben snapped as he launched a spray of dart-like diamonds towards Heatblast. He nodded in the direction of the guards. 'You and Grandpa get everyone else out of here.'

While Gwen and Grandpa led the guards to safety, a few more fireballs bounced off Diamondhead's body. He turned to face his attacker, only to discover the fake Heatblast had vanished.

'I don't know who you are,' Diamondhead

growled, his voice echoing around the inside of the Mint, 'but you're giving aliens a bad name.'

'So why don't you cry about it?' sneered Heatblast from somewhere close by. 'Or are you going to run and tell on me to your Grandpa Max, or that smart-mouth cousin of yours?'

Diamondhead stopped, stunned. His mind raced. How did this impostor know so much about his life? They'd never met before. Had they?

Suddenly, a blast of flame struck one of the trolleys that swung from the roof, carrying thousands of coins across the room. The metal casing exploded, and a stream of money poured down on Diamondhead, knocking him off his feet. As the hero tried to clamber free of the mountain of coins, Heatblast stepped out from behind a printing press.

'Hey, it's raining money!' he cried.

'Who are you?' Diamondhead demanded. Heatblast snorted.

'You still haven't figured it out?' he scoffed. 'Maybe this'll help.'

Before Diamondhead's eyes, the other alien's head began to change shape. First it stretched to look like XLR8. Next it became Ripjaws. It quickly went through every one of Ben's aliens, before stopping on a face that was chillingly familiar. This face was human. Or, at least, it used to be.

'*Kevin?*' Diamondhead gasped.

Ben had met Kevin earlier in the summer, and they'd quickly become friends. That is until Kevin stole Ben's powers and tried to kill a trainful of people. That kind of thing can break even the strongest of friendships.

Last time they'd fought, Ben had barely survived. This time, Kevin seemed to be more powerful than ever.

'I don't get it,' Diamondhead said, getting up to face his enemy. 'I thought you were drained of all my power back in the subway in New York.'

'That's what you get for thinking, Benji,' Kevin spat. 'Turns out I absorbed enough of the weird watch energy that I could turn into any of those aliens, if I just concentrated hard enough.' His eyes narrowed into thin slits. 'Only problem is now I can only stay human for a short time. You made me into this freak!'

'Like this is my fault?' Diamondhead growled. 'Whose idea was it to drain out all the powers of the watch? Not mine!'

'I don't care,' Kevin snarled, 'cos now it's payback time, "partner". Everything fifty-fifty. I do the crime and you'll do the time!'

'You'll never get away with this.'

'Wrong!' cried Kevin. 'You'll never get away with this! I'm not me. I'm you. Remember?'

A volley of laser fire brought one of the building's windows crashing in. A squad of Alien Containment Troops came clambering through.

'Keep the change!' Kevin grinned,

throwing a handful of coins at Diamondhead. 'You can use it to pay your bail.'

He gritted his teeth and concentrated. Within moments, he'd morphed into the insect-like Stinkfly.

'Gotta fly!' he hissed. Diamondhead could only watch as Stinkfly-Kevin sliced upwards and escaped through a hole in the Mint's glass ceiling.

A platoon of soldiers rushed to surround Diamondhead, their weapons trained on him.

Lieutenant Steel stepped between them, stopping directly in front of the captive alien.

'Sorry, rock-head,' he growled. 'No unauthorised withdrawals on my watch!'

CHAPTER THREE

RUNAWAY CABLE CAR

Diamondhead backed away from Steel, his eyes fixed on the gun the man held.

'You don't get it,' he protested. 'The bad alien just got away. I'm the good alien!'

'Yeah, sure you are. Just like those "alien heroes" all over the news nowadays.' Steel raised his weapon. 'No sale. To me you're just a walking chandelier.'

'He's telling the truth, officer,' said Gwen as she and Grandpa burst through the doors. 'There was another alien who –'

'I don't try 'em, kid; I just catch 'em.' Steel shrugged. 'We'll let the boys at Area Fifty-one figure out who's naughty and who's nice.'

Behind Steel, a dozen soldiers trained their weapons on Diamondhead.

'Chicago, Tallahassee, Barstow,' said the commander, counting off the cities on his fingers. 'You and your outer-space pals have been keeping me real busy, but you're not getting away with it this time.'

Diamondhead frowned. *This time?* What did he mean?

There was no time to think about it now. If he were going to escape, he had to act fast. With a flick of his wrist, he launched a handful of diamond missiles towards the Alien Containment Team. The deadly shards sliced through their laser guns, causing them to explode, spraying sparks and smoke in all directions.

Seizing his chance, Diamondhead ran through the thick, black plumes, dodging sprays of gunfire from those soldiers who still had weapons.

'Get that thing!' Steel roared, stabbing a finger in the fleeing alien's direction.

Diamondhead skidded round a corner and stopped by some heavy machinery. If he could find somewhere to hide, maybe he would change back to Ben before he was discovered. But when you're a giant alien made of green diamond finding a hiding place isn't easy.

A red dot appeared on his broad chest. He peered down at it, watching it shimmer back and forth just above his stomach. It was a few seconds before the terrible realisation hit him. The red dot was coming from a laser targeting system! Someone had him in their sights!

KRRR-ZZZAP! A crackling energy blast struck him hard. Its force slammed him down on to the ground. As the concrete floor shattered, it threw up a billowing cloud of dust, engulfing the fallen alien.

High up on a metal walkway, two soldiers exchanged a high five. They'd done it. They'd brought him down. They'd probably get a promotion for this.

A razor-sharp shard of diamond sliced through the air between them and embedded itself into the wall with a faint crack. The soldiers gulped nervously and peered over the edge of the railing. Diamondhead stood below, staring back up. He winked, before spraying several more shards of diamonds up towards the walkway.

The slivers of precious stone sliced through the metal railing, and both men soon found themselves tumbling to the ground below. They thudded down, one on top of the other. For a moment they thought about moving, but decided that staying where they were might be the safest option.

Footsteps clacked along the concrete somewhere behind Diamondhead. The alien turned, ready to fight, but a horribly familiar bleeping forced him to rethink his plans. The Omnitrix was flashing red. Any minute now he was going to change back!

Steel rounded the corner, gun raised and ready. His finger tightened on the trigger for a moment, before relaxing. Lowering his weapon, he glared down at the small boy cowering on the floor, his eyes tightly shut.

'Don't hurt me!' Ben begged. Slowly, he opened one eye. 'Oh,' he said, trying his best not to grin. 'Is that monster gone?'

* * *

'Oh, thank goodness you found him!' cried
Gwen, as Steel and the soldiers led Ben out into
the fresh air. 'We were so worried. He's always
wandering away. We're considering getting a
leash.'

Steel sighed and shoved Ben in the
direction of his waiting family. As he did, his
eyes fell on the Omnitrix.

'Nice watch,' he said. 'Never seen
anything like it.'

'Yeah,' Ben said, hiding it behind his back.
'It's from, ah . . . Japan.'

'No sign of the alien, sir,' announced a
soldier as he emerged from the Mint. 'It's like
that thing disappeared into thin air.'

Steel clenched his jaw, making the thick
muscles on his neck stand out. He glared at the
Tennysons. 'I don't suppose you three know
anything about this alien?'

'No,' said Grandpa Max quickly. 'If we did, we'd tell you.'

Steel's eyes narrowed. 'Yeah. Of course you would.'

The man performed a sharp about-turn and began marching away, much to Ben's relief. Talk about a narrow escape!

'Keep an eye on them,' Steel told a soldier, when they were out of the Tennysons' earshot. 'They know more than they're saying.'

❈ ❈ ❈

Back in The Rust Bucket, Ben filled Grandpa and Gwen in on everything he'd learned. Gwen's fingers flitted over the keys of her laptop as she listened. Ben could never understand how she managed to hold a conversation and type at the same time. If he were honest, it kind of creeped him out.

'It was Kevin at both the video-game

store and the Mint,' Ben told them. 'They were set-ups!'

'That would explain a lot,' said Grandpa with a nod. 'I don't mind telling you, that kid's rowboat is missing a couple of paddles.'

'But why does the swat-team guy think all aliens are bad?' asked Ben.

'Looks like from personal experience,' said Gwen. 'Check this out.'

She spun the laptop round, revealing a scanned newspaper article. The photograph showed Ripjaws attacking a group of panicked civilians. 'Your friend has been busy,' Gwen continued. 'And not just here in San Francisco. Wildmutt terrorising Tallahassee. Ripjaws in Chicago. Ghostfreak in Barstow . . .'

'I'm going to get blamed for all that stuff,' Ben cried. 'And I didn't do any of it!'

Suddenly, a loud grinding noise coming from outside caught their attention. All three occupants of The Rust Bucket huddled together to peer through a side window. What they saw chilled them to the bone.

One of San Francisco's famous trams – a vehicle pulled along the streets by a thick underground steel rope – was speeding down a steep hill. Inside, the passengers screamed, trapped and helpless. Outside, the normally red cable car shone with a black-and-green alien sheen.

'Kevin!' Ben spat.

'The boy must've gone Upgrade to hijack that tram,' Grandpa gasped.

Ben leaped up from his seat and adjusted the Omnitrix. 'Anything he can upgrade, I can upgrade better!'

With a blinding flash of green, Ben transformed. He felt the rough fur covering his body and groaned.

'Wildmutt?' snorted Gwen. 'Nice choice, Fido.'

The alien canine gave a yelp of frustration before throwing open the door of the motorhome and bounding along the street after the cable car.

Up on a nearby rooftop, an Alien Containment soldier pressed the button on the side of his walkie-talkie. 'Mobile One. A wild-dog alien just emerged from the motorhome. Now both are heading down California Street.'

Steel's voice hissed over the radio. 'Maintain visual. I'm on my way.'

Inside the speeding tram, the driver struggled with the brake lever. Behind him, terrified tourists screamed and clawed at the windows, desperately trying to escape.

'Now why are you doing that?' said a voice from the front of the car. Two snaking coils unfolded from the dashboard. They wrapped round the brake lever, wrenched it from the driver's grasp, and snapped it in half. 'We're just starting to have fun!'

THUD! Wildmutt landed on the roof of the tram. Almost at once, the metal below his feet rearranged itself to form Upgrade's face. 'Sorry, Ben,' Kevin cackled. 'No pets allowed!'

A large metal spike exploded upwards from the roof, stabbing into Wildmutt's paws. The dog-like alien howled with pain and leaped sideways. His sharp claws dug deep into the side of the tram, enabling him to swing in through the driver's window. **CRASH!**

The screaming tourists screamed even louder when they saw the savage beast come clattering through the window. The noise dazed Wildmutt, overwhelming his alien senses, and he didn't notice the two heavy benches until they were slammed down hard on his head.

'Heel, boy, heel!' laughed Upgrade-Kevin, as he stared down at his trapped foe. 'There's a good hero!'

Concentrating hard, Kevin released his control over the tram and returned to normal

Upgrade form on the roof. From there, he could see the rapidly approaching San Francisco Bay. Any minute now, the people in the tram would be going for their last swim.

'Let's see,' he muttered. 'Brakes are out, hero's trapped and everyone's about to go for a dip in the bay.' Groaning with the pain of the effort, Kevin morphed into Stinkfly and buzzed into the sky. 'I'd say my work here is done!'

CHAPTER FOUR

CLASH OF THE TITANS

WOOOOOSH! The Rust Bucket roared along the street, its hidden jet engines fully unfolded and engaged. Grandpa grinned, enjoying the thrill of the chase.

'Times like these my demolition derby experience really comes in handy!'

He eased down on the brake as they caught up with the runaway tram. Leaning out of his window, Grandpa Max pointed at a cable and hook, which were attached to the back of the tram.

'Ben, attach the line to the bottom of the motorhome!' he cried.

Wildmutt clambered out of the back of the

tram and took the metal hook in his powerful jaws. With a short bound, he landed on The Rust Bucket. It took him just a moment to set the hook in place.

Gwen gripped her seat as Grandpa slammed down hard on the brakes. Smoke poured from the tyres as the line tying the two vehicles together became tight. It wasn't enough though. The tram was still hurtling towards the water, and now it was dragging The Rust Bucket along with it! There were only seconds left until they all took the plunge.

One chance. They still had one chance! Grandpa Max flicked a switch on the dashboard then clamped his hands down on the steering wheel. Things were about to get scary.

With a hiss, a gas-propelled anchor launched from the back of The Rust Bucket. It rocketed backwards along the street before punching a hole straight through the side of a building. Wide metal prongs sprang out, locking the device in place.

Gwen screamed as the anchor line pulled tight. The sudden stop threw her forward, and only her safety belt stopped her crashing through the front windscreen.

When she'd recovered, Gwen raised her head enough to look out through the window. Up ahead, at the other end of the metal rope, stood the cable car. Its front end dangled dangerously out over the water, but everyone inside was safe.

They'd done it! They'd foiled Kevin's plan just in the nick of time.

A few minutes later, when both vehicles had been untangled, Grandpa and Gwen found Ben hiding round a corner. He'd only just transformed back from Wildmutt, and was still wiping the dust from his hands.

Gwen smiled at him. 'Not bad for an alien with no thumbs,' she admitted.

'Freeze!' barked a voice from behind them. The Tennysons turned to find themselves surrounded by the Special Alien Containment Team. Lieutenant Steel snarled as he stepped forward. 'One move and you're all Swiss cheese.'

Grandpa, Gwen and Ben all took a step back, half-blinded by the spotlight being shone down on them from a helicopter that circled above.

'You have two choices,' Steel warned them. 'Tell me what you have to do with these aliens, or get measured for your prison uniforms.' He caught Ben's arm and examined the Omnitrix. 'It has something to do with this watch, doesn't it?' Steel demanded. 'Is it some kind of signal to call the aliens?'

'Sir!' cried the nearest soldier. 'We're getting reports of a crystal alien rampaging on the Golden Gate. Looks like it could bring the whole bridge down if it isn't stopped.'

Steel hesitated. These people knew something, he was sure. Still, the alien had to be stopped before he could cause any more damage. 'Falcon One,' he said into his radio. 'Pick me up.' Overhead, the helicopter swung round on his command. The lieutenant glared down at Ben. 'We're not done.'

Watching the soldiers jump into the helicopter, Ben spun the dial on the Omnitrix. 'Those guys don't stand a chance against Kevin,' he said. '*I* have to stop him!'

✹ ✹ ✹

High on the vast metal supports of the Golden Gate Bridge, Kevin was hard at work. He had transformed into Diamondhead, and was using the alien's sharp hands to slice through the cables holding the giant construction together.

Down below, the road began to sway more and more with each cable Kevin sliced. Soon it would collapse completely, sending hundreds of innocent people tumbling to their doom.

A wind whipped at the villain from nowhere. He looked up and saw the SACT helicopter swooping down towards him. Lieutenant Steel hung below it, winching himself down to face the alien menace.

Kevin responded with a volley of diamond missiles. They clipped the tail of the helicopter, sending it into an uncontrollable spin.

'All right!' he cheered, as he watched the aircraft plunge towards the road below.

Swinging wildly, Steel sliced the rope that held him. He fell, hand reaching for his pistol, and landed on top of the metal support, directly in front of a startled Kevin.

Down below, the helicopter thwacked into the road. Luckily, some of the cables had slowed its fall, and all of the soldiers tumbled out, unhurt.

'Lieutenant Steel,' Kevin growled. 'So nice to see you again.'

❋ ❋ ❋

The Rust Bucket weaved past a squad of police cars and sped on to the swaying bridge. All around it, people screamed and fled in the opposite direction, trying to get clear before the structure gave way.

Ben leaped from the motorhome. He sighed when he saw the damage that had already been done to the bridge.

'Just one more thing I'm going to get blamed for!'

�֍ �֍ ✖

Lieutenant Steel flew backwards and slammed solidly against part of the metal structure. He dropped to his knees, fighting for breath. His face was a mass of cuts and bruises. He was losing the fight. Badly.

Diamondhead-Kevin reached down and jerked the officer off the ground. He held him against the main bridge support and pulled back his other arm, ready to deliver one final, devastating punch.

'Let him go, Kevin!'

Kevin turned, Steel still held in one hand. Four Arms crouched on top of the next support pillar, poised and ready for action. 'This is about you and me,' the hero growled.

Kevin shrugged. 'Sounds good to me.' He hurled his limp prisoner away. Steel threw out his hands, barely managing to catch hold of a cable. Muscles burning from the effort, he pulled himself up on to a narrow platform and waited for his strength to return.

'Still trying to be a goody two shoes, Ben?' Kevin snickered. 'Let me guess – you just want to *help* me.'

'You had plenty of chances to get help, but you always messed it up.' Four Arms narrowed both pairs of yellow eyes. 'This time, you're getting what you deserve.'

'Aww, does this mean we're not best buddies any more?' said Kevin sarcastically. He cackled maniacally as he unleashed a spray of diamonds in Four Arms' direction.

The big red alien somersaulted over the attack and landed at his enemy's feet.

KA-RUNCH! A powerful uppercut sent Kevin crashing backwards into a support pillar.

'You risked all those innocent lives just to get even with me!' snapped Four Arms, advancing.

'Nobody's innocent!' Kevin screeched, jumping to his feet. 'They just haven't had a chance to make fun of me yet!'

Down beside the wreckage of the

helicopter, two soldiers took aim with the Concussion Bazooka. Their sights were trained on the aliens, who were now locked in battle.

'You can't do this!' Gwen protested. 'He's trying to help!'

'Targets locked on, sir,' barked the trooper into his radio. 'Permission to fire?'

Steel opened his swollen eyes and watched the aliens clashing violently. Something was different about the red one. Something he wasn't quite sure of. He unclipped his walkie-talkie from his belt.

'Fire on my command only,' he said. 'Repeat. On my command only.'

Four Arms ducked a swinging punch and caught Diamondhead-Kevin by the throat. With a grunt of effort he yanked the villain into the air, before slamming him down hard on to the ground.

Kevin's body instantly began to morph. A jet of flame shot up from his fingers as he

changed into Heatblast. The fire hit Four Arms in the face, temporarily blinding him.

Eyes stinging, Four Arms lashed out. A flailing fist caught Heatblast-Kevin as he stood up, sending him soaring into the sky. Changing so quickly was difficult – and painful – but Kevin managed to transform into Stinkfly and slow himself down.

The insect alien looped twice to build up speed, then rocketed down towards the still half-blinded Four Arms. He was going to knock the hero right off the edge, and end this thing once and for all!

CHAPTER FIVE

ALL CHANGE

As Kevin swooped down towards Four Arms, something began to happen to him. A sharp, shooting pain coursed through his body. His pincer-like claws shrank and altered, twisting into five stubby fingers. His wings stopped flapping and curled down into his body.

And then suddenly, in a blur of limbs, he changed completely. Several hundred feet above sea level, he cried out in horror as he realised he was no longer Stinkfly-Kevin. Nor was he Heatblast-Kevin. He wasn't even Diamondhead-Kevin. He was just Kevin, plain and simple. And he was falling fast!

BA-DOING! The tumbling Kevin struck

Four Arms on the chest and bounced off. The big red alien peered down at the eleven-year-old boy who lay in a crumpled heap at his feet. Roaring, Four Arms threw two of his arms above his head, then swung them back down. His fists connected with a deafening BOOM!

Cowering, Kevin flicked open one eye. On either side of his head, deep fist-shaped dents had been hammered into the metal. He opened the other eye and raised his head. Four Arms was walking away, the battle – as far as he was concerned – well and truly over.

'Get back here and fight, Tennyson,' Kevin cried. 'I'm not through with you yet!'

Four Arms paused. 'But I'm through with you,' he said, his voice as dry and coarse as gravel. 'You're not worth it. You never were.'

Kevin scrambled back up, his face contorting in rage. How dare Tennyson speak to him like that? Everyone always made fun of him. Everyone called him a freak. There was no way he was letting Ben walk away. No way!

The hatred and the fury burned through Kevin's veins. As they did, another transformation began to take place. He gasped as something seemed to explode inside him, pushing his chest forwards and forcing his shoulders out.

Kevin threw back his head and tried to scream, but a terrible, inhuman roar burst from his lips, which had become bloated and cracked. The skin on his back blistered and split as two Stinkfly wings emerged. Kevin wasn't changing into the insect alien though. He was changing into . . . something else. Something *new*.

Four Arms watched in horror as Kevin continued to mutate. A Wildmutt arm grew from the villain's ribs. Then a Diamondhead arm sprouted from his shoulder. His legs, too, became as red and muscled as Four Arms' own. A long, tapered XLR8 tail snaked down from the base of his spine.

Most hideous of all, however, was his
face. Nothing about it was Kevin's. Instead,
it was a patchwork quilt of mismatched eyes,
jagged teeth and spindly antennae.

Kevin clenched his fists and concentrated,
desperately trying to change back, desperately
trying to be normal.

'I-I can't change back!' he wailed at last.
'I'm . . . I'm stuck like this!' He rounded on Four
Arms, his massive frame towering over the
heroic alien. 'Look at what you've done!' he
bellowed.

Oh, man, thought Ben. *Is there anything I'm not going to get blamed for today?*

A thunderous punch to the head brought his train of thought crashing to a halt. Kevin drove a knee sharply into Four Arms' stomach, knocking the wind from his body. A lightning-fast tail whipped round, knocking the hero's feet from under him.

Four of the strongest arms in the planet stretched out, as the alien tried desperately to catch on to the bridge. He tumbled backwards over the edge, plummeting towards certain doom.

One hand finally found something to grab. With a jerk, Four Arms came to an sudden stop, dangling more than two hundred metres above the water. A shadow loomed over him as Kevin shambled over to the edge.

'You'll never beat me,' Kevin snarled. 'Because you're one of the good guys. And good guys never have the guts to finish guys like me!'

'But I do!' barked Lieutenant Steel from the nearby ledge. He jabbed his finger against the button on his walkie-talkie and yelled: 'Fire!'

The blast of the Concussion Bazooka scorched up through the air, covering the distance from the bottom of the bridge to the top in a heartbeat. The beam drove Kevin backwards. He thrashed frantically, but was too late to stop himself falling. Watched by dozens of onlookers, Kevin dropped from the bridge, and plummeted into the icy cold waters below.

Four Arms dragged himself up on to the bridge and leaped across to where Lieutenant Steel was struggling upright. The soldier glared at the hulking alien, but made no move to attack.

'Are you still looking for me?' asked Four Arms.

'Second target locked on,' crackled a voice over the walkie-talkie. 'Permission to fire?'

Steel hesitated, the radio held close to his mouth. The events of the last few minutes were a painful blur, but he reckoned he could pretty much piece together what had been happening.

'We got our alien,' he said. 'Stand down.'

Four Arms nodded. That was exactly what he'd been hoping to hear. With a twitch of his gigantic legs, the alien bounded off across the bridge, making his getaway before the watch decided to time out on him again.

Steel leaned forwards and peered over the

edge. The ground seemed a long way away.

'Well, what are you waiting for?' he barked into his radio. 'Pretty please? Get me down!'

❈ ❈ ❈

Twenty minutes later, all three Tennysons strapped themselves into their usual seats in The Rust Bucket. Every part of Ben ached. He was going to be covered in bruises for a week! Still, at least they were all out of danger. For now.

'Not even Kevin could have survived that blast and that fall,' said Gwen. 'Right?'

'You're asking the wrong guy,' Ben sighed. 'I thought he was gone for good last time.'

Grandpa slipped the motorhome into gear and began to pull out into the slow moving procession of traffic. A bruised and battered figure in military uniform stepped in front, blocking the way. Steel approached the passenger window and rapped hard on the glass.

'Now why is it,' he began, when Ben wound down the window, 'that you three are always around when aliens show up?'

'Really,' said Grandpa, 'is that a fact? We hadn't noticed.'

'Yeah, guess it's just coincidence,' replied Steel suspiciously, his eyes narrowed. He stepped back from the motorhome, making room for it to pass. 'Maybe we'll cross paths again some time. Drive carefully. Lots of weird stuff out there.'

Ben grinned. 'Yeah,' he said. 'You're telling us!'

Steel watched The Rust Bucket drive away, weaving past police cars and burning wreckage as it headed off the bridge, and towards whatever adventure awaited it.

In the water beneath the bridge, unseen by any of the people above, a cluster of bubbles rose to the surface and burst.

Something was down there – and it was
still very much alive . . .